THE BIG BAZOOHLEY

WEEKLY READER BOOK CLUB PRESENTS

THE BIG BAZOOHLEY

PETER CAREY

ILLUSTRATIONS BY

ABIRA ALI

A John Macrae Book

HENRY HOLT AND COMPANY

NEW YORK

This book is a presentation of Newfield Publications, Inc.
Newfield Publications offers book clubs for children from
preschool through high school. For further information
write to: **Newfield Publications, Inc.,** 4343 Equity Drive,
Columbus, Ohio 43228.

Published by arrangement with Henry Holt and Company, Inc.
Newfield Publications is a federally registered
trademark of Newfield Publications, Inc.
Weekly Reader is a federally registered trademark
of Weekly Reader Corporation.

1996 edition

Henry Holt and Company, Inc.
Publishers since 1866
115 West 18th Street
New York, New York 10011

Henry Holt is a registered
trademark of Henry Holt and Company, Inc.

Library of Congress Cataloging-in-Publication Data
Carey, Peter. The big Bazoohley/Peter Carey; pictures by Abira Ali.
p. cm.
"A John Macrae book."
Summary: When his family runs low on funds while on a trip to Toronto,
nine-year-old Sam, hoping to win $10,000, allows himself to be "borrowed"
and entered in a contest to find the Perfecto Kiddo.
[1. Parent and child—Fiction. 2. Luck—Fiction. 3. Contests—
Fiction. 4. Toronto (Ont.)—Fiction.] I. Ali, Abira, ill. II. Title.
PZ7.C21432Bi 1995 [Fic]—dc20 95-15282

ISBN 0-8050-3855-8

First Edition—1995

Printed in the United States of America

For Sam Carey and Charley Summers

THE BIG BAZOOHLEY

ONE

LIKE MOST GROWN-UPS, Sam Kellow's parents never guessed that their son ever thought about money. Like most grown-ups, they thought he did not appreciate its value, and they both liked to say things to him like "Money doesn't grow on trees" and "If you knew how much that cost, you wouldn't do that."

But in truth Sam knew a lot about how much things cost, and when the family arrived in Toronto in the middle of a blizzard, he knew they were there to sell his mother's latest painting to the mysterious Mr. Edward St. John de Vere. He also knew they were down to their last fifty-three dollars and twenty cents.

KING EDWARD
TAXI

Sam was only nine years old but he had a brain like a computer. He could add, subtract, do five-number long division in his head. He knew what sort of a hotel you could stay in for fifty-three dollars and twenty cents, and it certainly wasn't a hotel like the one his father drove up to. The moment Sam saw the King Redward Hotel looming up through the snowstorm he got a very bad feeling in his stomach. When he saw the doorman, with all his gold buttons and medals on his big black coat, he knew this was a very expensive hotel and he felt even sicker.

What if his mother could not sell the painting she was carrying with her? What if the mysterious Mr. de Vere had died, or had been called away on business, or saw his mother's new painting and didn't like the faces on the people or the color of the sky?

They would be stuck in this hotel with a big bill and no money.

But even while Sam was worrying, his father was smiling and throwing his car keys to the doorman. His father was a gambler. In other words, he made all his money (or lost all his money) by guessing which horse would win a race, which playing card would turn up on the top of the deck, which drop of rain would run fastest down a windowpane. Money never bothered him, not ever. People said of Earl Kellow that he was the sort of man who would give you his last dollar, and although Sam was proud of his father, this also made him very nervous.

When they traveled to a strange city, Sam never knew whether they would be living on peanut butter sandwiches or sitting in a fancy restaurant being served that famous, fabulous, flaming ice-cream cake called Bombe Alaska.

He never knew whether they would stay in a palace or a fleapit, and in fact Sam knew plenty of both, and now that he was nine he knew which he liked better.

He watched his father tip the doorman five dollars and the bell captain two dollars, and when the porter brought their single suitcase to the room, Sam saw how much Earl Kellow gave him and he knew they now had only forty-four dollars and twenty cents left in all the world.

Sam looked at his mother to see if she was worried, and she looked down at him and smiled. He could not tell.

People were always telling Sam what a handsome woman his mother was, as if he never noticed himself. She was as tall as his father. She had big feet and hands and wild, curling blond hair and a pair of eyes which were different colors, the left bluish and the right brownish.

Her name was Vanessa and you might think—looking at those size-ten feet and those hands—that she would paint paintings as big as a dining-room table, but no—her paintings were no bigger than a matchbox.

No one ever explained how Vanessa Kellow could do it, how *anyone* could do it, and even if she had been two feet tall, you would have considered it a miracle. For these tiny paintings showed entire cities. Not just the buildings and the streets, but the bakers and butchers, and the stews bubbling in the pots, and the freckles on the faces, and the cat sleeping in the basket, and the fluff under the beds, although you could not see these things without a special magnifying glass, and then you might find a ruby ring in a secret drawer or a jar of blue-and-green-striped candy in a cupboard, and even then you would have the feeling that there were many things, things that were there, that you could not see.

People would go crazy when they saw his mother's tiny paintings. They just had to own them, straight-away, and if they were rich people, they would pay a lot of money for the privilege. The only problem was, it took a whole year to do one little painting.

And it was one of these paintings, wrapped in tissue paper in her purse, that she was about to deliver. The minute they came into the hotel room, his mother set about fitting the painting inside a little box and then wrapping it in gold paper.

"Wow," his father said, looking out the window of the hotel room. "Look at that city. Look at all that snow."

His father loved new cities, new games, new people to gamble with. Sam did not understand why they couldn't stay at

home in Australia and just gamble there. Instead the family traveled the world, from race course to race course, from casino to casino, from Sydney to Paris to Tokyo to London to Toronto, seeking what his father called the Big Bazoohley, which meant the Big Win, the Big Prize, the Jackpot.

Sometimes he got the Big Bazoohley and sometimes he did not, but in any case he was tall and handsome and fun to be with, even when he lost. He could balance a dining chair on his nose and find pennies behind your ears. He had bright blue eyes and he could play cricket and baseball, and wherever they traveled there was something about him that made people like him and lend him money when he had none of his own.

Sam stood beside his father and watched the snow come down. The flakes were huge, and the fall was dense. The snow blew in swirls and eddies. It stuck to the window ledge and filled the ledge, and as they watched, it began to creep up the glass as if it meant to pull a soft white blanket over the face of the hotel.

"Gee, it's beautiful," his father said. Sam would have agreed if he knew that they could stay inside where it was warm and safe, but he couldn't look out the window. He looked instead at the expensive gold-framed mirrors, at the big sunken bath, at the forty-eight-inch TV, at the perfect green grapes in the glistening silver bowl.

"How will Mum get to her appointment?" he asked his father. "Maybe she won't be able to get there in all of this snow."

"This is Toronto," his father said. "This is a great city in the snow. They have a wonderful subway system. They have shopping centers underground. And as a matter of fact, Mr. de Vere has a mansion which is totally underground. You reach it from a door on the Bloor Street subway platform."

Sam was too worried about his mother to think it strange that a rich man would have his front door on a subway platform. He looked out the window. The snow was falling so fast now. It lay itself on the roofs below and all the streets and made everything soft and curved and white and quiet. In all that great city nothing was moving but the flashing yellow lights on the top of the snowplows.

"But how will she get to the subway?"

"I'll take the hotel elevator," his mother said. She stood in the middle of the room with the tiny gold-wrapped painting held in the palm of her hand. "The

Bloor and Yonge lines run through the hotel basement. Neat, huh?"

"Neat," said Sam, but when his father wanted him to go out and sled and play in the snow, he said he would rather stay in the room, and so, when his mother left, Sam and his dad stayed in the room and they watched the cartoon channel and after a while Sam stood and went to the door, where he tried to see, without being obvious, how much this hotel room was costing.

Four hundred and fifty-three dollars a night. Plus tax.

TWO

SAM'S MOTHER DID NOT get back until it was dark, and when she came into the hotel room, she had a funny look on her face.

"So?" his father said. He walked toward his wife with his arms wide. "Do we celebrate now or later? Do we order the Bombe Alaska? Do we put on our dancing shoes, or what?"

"Excuse me," Vanessa said, and she ducked sideways into the bathroom, where Sam could hear her blowing her nose. When she finally came out, she still had a funny look on her face.

Sam got a bad feeling in his stomach. He lay on the big king-size bed with the carved gold headboard and pretended to watch the television.

His mother sat down on the sofa beside his father.

"So?" Earl Kellow asked quietly.

"De Vere wasn't there," his mother said.

Sam saw his father's shoulders shrug. "He'll come back."

"*It* wasn't there," his mother whispered. "Nothing was there. The entrance to the mansion wasn't there anymore."

Sam saw his father take his mother's hand and begin to stroke it. He said something Sam could not hear.

"Earl," Vanessa said. "I've been there five times before. I know the station. I know the entrance."

"It's the door that says 'Cleaning 201.' " He turned to Sam. "Crazy old de Vere," he said. "Richest man in Toronto and he writes 'Cleaning 201' on his front door."

"Earl," Vanessa said, "I know what it says. The sign wasn't there. The *door* wasn't there. What I'm trying to tell you is—the whole station has been rebuilt."

"Maybe you got out at Wellesley instead. Or Dundas."

Vanessa whispered something short and sharp in her husband's ear.

"Okay," Earl said, "maybe I will."

"Suit yourself," Vanessa said.

"Sam," his father said, "will you go down and wait for

me in the lobby? I just want to talk to Mummy for two minutes."

"Sure," Sam said, but he could see his father was worried, and that made him feel really bad.

So Sam went down in the elevator to the lobby and sat in a deep upholstered chair beside a fountain. The lobby was tall and grand with sparkling chandeliers and Oriental rugs. Grown-ups in big fur coats came in the front door laughing and talking excitedly while the snow melted on their soft black hats. A porter in a uniform walked past holding a huge blue-and-yellow parrot in a gold cage. A girl of six with very white skin and a long silver ball gown was speaking seriously to an older boy, a sixth grader at least, dressed in a black tuxedo.

As they walked past Sam, he heard the boy say excitedly, "He's sick? He's really sick?"

And the girl giggled behind her hand and said, "Ten thousand dollars says he is."

Sam wished he had ten thousand dollars.

Then his father arrived and silently he held out his hand. Sam did not ask what his mother and father had talked about. He stood and walked hand in hand with his father across the lobby. They passed six cashiers, all

standing in a line behind a shining mahogany desk. The cashiers wore black suit jackets and had black slicked-back hair. Sam felt that they could tell that Sam and his dad did not have the money to pay the bill.

Just beyond the cashiers there was another elevator, which went to the parking lots and the King Street subway station.

When they stepped out of the elevator, there was a token booth.

"I don't have to pay," Sam whispered. "I can duck under."

"You can do no such thing," his father said.

"Why not?"

"Because it's cheating."

When they pushed through the turnstile, they had forty-one dollars and seventy cents left.

Two minutes later the train arrived. Sam, who had spent the week before in New York City, was surprised by how clean and quiet it was. Five minutes later they arrived at Bloor Street.

Sam's father led the way along the northbound platform.

"You said there was a whole house in there? In the subway?"

“You wait till we find him. He looks kind of like a mole.”

“He has tunnels?”

“He has a mansion under here. There’s a marble fountain just inside the door. There is a ballroom, and galleries with paintings worth millions of dollars.”

"But why does Mr. de Vere live here?"

"When you're very rich," his father said, "you can live any way or anywhere you like. Eddie de Vere is a funny little mole of a guy, not much taller than you are. He is a very big gambler, but he's also very shy, and he doesn't want people to know he is rich. He walks around the street in old overalls carrying a plastic bucket and then comes down to the subway and opens the door marked CLEANING 201. He likes secrets. That's why he loves your Mum's paintings. There's so much more in them than you think when you first glance at them."

"Like him?"

"I guess," his father said. "But who knows what he thinks." He was standing in front of an advertisement for M&M's, running his hands over the picture. "This is very strange . . ." he said. His voice trailed off. He was frowning.

"So?" Sam asked. He had never seen his father look so worried before.

"I'm darned if I know," his father said. He put the tips of his fingers behind the sign and pulled at it. "The door used to be here, but it's not here now." He paused and rubbed his ear. "They've been rebuilding. . . ."

"It can't be just *gone,*" said Sam, looking at the big bright M&M's in front of him.

"Sam, I'm telling you, they've rebuilt the station. They've blocked up the doorway."

"They've put the doorway someplace else."

"Yes, I guess they have." Sam's father looked up and down the bright shining white-tiled wall. There was not another door in sight.

"Maybe he's in there still," Sam said. "Maybe he's on the other side of the wall. Maybe he would hear us if we knocked the right way. Maybe there's a code. Maybe we should push on one of these M&M's."

His father shrugged.

Sam smacked the picture of the M&M's with his hands.

"So what will happen to us?" Sam said. He began to cry. It was all too much. "What will happen to us now? Where will we get our money? How will we pay for the hotel?"

"Well," his father said, "I'll tell you what . . ."

And he picked Sam up and held him in the air, and Sam looked at his father's face and saw how he smiled and how calm he was.

"I'll tell you what," his father said, hugging him.

"What?" Sam was smiling, too. He could see his father knew just what to do.

"One thing I've found out in life is one door shuts, another door opens."

He put Sam down.

"Which door opens?" Sam said. "Where?"

But his father shrugged and held out his hand. "Come on," he said. "Let's go back and see your mum."

But Sam didn't move. He looked into his father's eyes and saw Earl Kellow did not know what to do.

"You're lying!" he yelled. "You don't know anything. You're lying. You don't know what to do."

His father tried to hug him, but Sam was angry and would not let him.

Finally he took his father's hand and walked with him up and down the platforms, looking for the door marked CLEANING 201. As they walked the busy corridors of the Queen Street station, Sam was still angry and upset and it never occurred to him that what his father had said might actually come true.

Before midnight another door would open. And Sam would walk right through it.

THREE

SAM WAS SURPRISED, when they got off the train, to find they were at a station called Osgoode.

When they went up in the elevator, he found, not a hotel lobby with chandeliers, but a huge supermarket. When he saw the supermarket, Sam's heart fell. He knew what they were buying—peanut butter, bread, milk. That's how he knew his father was defeated. It was what he always bought when he had no money.

His father spent six dollars and ten cents at the supermarket. Which meant he had thirty-five dollars and sixty cents to pay for the hotel bill. And yet Earl Kellow didn't seem to worry, and when he spent another two

fifty on two tokens to get back to the hotel, he was whistling.

Back in the hotel the lobby looked even grander than it had before. There was a famous film star checking in. There was a pretty fifth grader in a ballerina gown with a diamond tiara in her hair. She looked beautiful, like a real-life princess. She looked at Sam and smiled, but Sam—instead of smiling back—frowned and shifted his supermarket bag so she wouldn't see the peanut butter showing through the plastic.

As he walked across the marble floor, he imagined everyone was looking at his pathetic little bag of groceries—cashiers, bellboys, a pair of twin boys in identical brown velvet suits and neat bow ties.

"There's a lot of very rich people staying here," he whispered to his father.

"These kids?" His father laughed. "They're pretending to be like the kids in those shampoo commercials. Did you see the sign?"

Sam looked at the banner which was now draped

across the high ceiling of the lobby. It read: THE KING REDWARD HOTEL WELCOMES FINALISTS IN THE PERFECTO SHAMPOO "PERFECTO KIDDO" COMPETITION.

"Perfecto Kiddo," Sam said. "It's not even English. It doesn't make sense."

"Why would it make sense, kiddo?" Earl Kellow grinned. "It's a nonsensical situation. It's a whole lot of crazy parents trying to make money from their children."

"But they have jewels and stuff," Sam whispered. "Why do they need more money?"

"They're not rich, Sam. The parents are dressing the kids up in an unnatural way so they can make money from them."

Sam turned his baseball hat around backward and pushed his hands deliberately in his pockets. He acted proud, but he would rather have been in their shiny shoes than his dirty sneakers. He felt ashamed of his sloppy sweater, his crumpled jeans, his baseball cap. These kids would still be hanging around the lobby when he was kicked out of the hotel.

In the elevator his father said, "You thought *your* life was strange, huh?"

"Yes," said Sam, but he could not think what else to

say. He just wanted to sleep, to forget everything. He ate his peanut butter sandwich and drank his milk. He cleaned his teeth and kissed his mum good night.

"You want a story, sweetheart?" she asked.

"Unh-uh."

"You want to read yourself?"

"Unh-uh. I'm tired."

"Okay, but take off your Blue Jays cap before you go to sleep."

Sam began to dream immediately, his cap still backward on his head.

FOUR

In Sam's dream, he was back at the Bloor Street platform, in front of the M&M's advertisement. He was there because he was going to find Mr. de Vere. He stretched out his hand to the advertisement, and as he touched the big bright red M&M, the poster swung open, like a door.

At first he thought it was a closet. He could see a cleaner's mop and a bucket of smelly water. Then, as he listened to the noise of water dripping, he knew he was at the entrance to a long dark hallway. He could smell wet earth and see spiderwebs, but he knew that he had no choice but to go in there. He knew he was the only one who could find Mr. de Vere.

At first he had to fight his way through a forest of brooms and mops, and then he had to push aside a great pile of cleaner's rags.

After he got past the rags he found himself in a long smooth hallway with low soft yellow lights. There were small neat cubbyholes set into the wall at regular intervals. They were like display cases in a museum, and in each one there was a small silver bowl filled with M&M's.

Sam took a single M&M and ate it.

Someone said, "It's magic."

Indeed this M&M did not taste like any M&M's he had ever tasted. It was filled with something sweet and runny and golden, like honey, but much, much nicer.

When he looked again the light in the corridor had become golden, and beautiful paintings had appeared on the walls. The carpet on the floor was deep and soft. He knelt down to feel it. When he stood again the hallway had changed once more.

The paintings had disappeared. Where the paintings had been there were small round windows like portholes in a ship. As he peered into a porthole he realized that he could see Mr. de Vere's secret mansion.

On the other side of the little windows he could see

Mr. de Vere himself. He was dressed in a red smoking jacket and gold slippers and he was looking at a beetle with a magnifying glass.

Sam began to hurry along the hallway, looking for an entrance.

"I'm Sam!" he shouted. "Vanessa Kellow's son."

Mr. de Vere seemed to have forgotten his beetle. He was walking along beside Sam, on the other side of the wall. He was nodding his head and his long mole-like nose was creased in a smile. "The door is just ahead," he called. "Go down the slide and into the tunnel."

And then suddenly it was dark.

"What slide?"

"Just keep walking, you'll find it."

Sam took another step, tripped, and then he felt himself falling. He was in a dark, soft, gloomy place. It felt like the cleaner's closet again, but now a television was playing.

"That's right," Mr. de Vere's voice called. "Now just walk in the door."

Sam could not find any door. He was in a sea of cleaner's rags. "What door?" he called.

"For heaven's sake," Mr. de Vere snapped impatiently, "are you an imbecile? Do you want the money or don't you?"

"My father wants it, too," Sam said. "It isn't just me."

"Can't even find a door!"

"I can," said Sam. "I really can." And it was at that moment that Sam found a door handle. He grasped it. He turned it. He pulled, and the big brown door swung smoothly toward him.

It was with a feeling of enormous relief that Sam walked into the long, luxurious, carpeted hallway with little yellow lights along the wall and a big arrangement of dried flowers and a huge gold mirror at the end.

Sam blinked and looked around. It took a good minute for him to realize that he had been dreaming. Indeed it was only after he had heard the door swing shut behind him that he realized that he had sleepwalked out of his hotel room.

He was locked out.

FIVE

SAM KELLOW HAD WALKED into the hallway. And when he tried to get back into the hotel room, he found it locked against him.

He knocked on the door. But the door was black and hard and although he hit it with all his might, his small fist made precious little noise.

He put his ear against the door. All he could hear was thick dead wood.

Okay, he thought, what now?

The answer was obvious: get in the elevator, go downstairs to reception, ask them to let him in his room.

Sam looked down at his faded Sonic the Hedgehog

pajamas, the ones his mum had given him when he turned eight years old. They were too short in the legs. They were torn on the shoulder. The truth was, he looked like someone whose parents couldn't pay the bill, and he would rather have died than go downstairs and be stared at by people in fur coats.

So he went to the next door along the corridor instead. He knocked once, then twice. He put his ear to the door. All he could hear was the sound of wood.

He turned his baseball cap the right way on his head. He went to the next door and he knocked, not with his knuckles this time, but with the flat of his hand. He kicked the door. He put his mouth against the door. "Yo!" he called. He took his baseball cap off and smoothed his hair. Then he put his mouth close to the door again. "I'm locked out of my room."

And then, like a miracle, he heard distant *life* on the other side of the door—a noise like leaves rustling, papers being shuffled, or perhaps a pair of leather slippers on a wooden floor.

"Who's that?" The wheezy, phlegmy old voice was so close it made him jump.

"It's only me."

"Who is 'me'?"

"I'm Sam."

"What do you want, 'Sam'? What brings you knocking on my door at midnight?"

"I'm locked out of my room."

"How do I know you're not a robber come to take my money?"

"I'm just a kid."

"That's what you say. I can't *see* you."

"Don't I sound like a kid?"

"You might be a ventriloquist," said the voice on the other side of the door. "This hotel is full of kids who don't look like kids."

"There's a competition," Sam said. "The Perfecto Kiddo competition."

"Those were not kids," the wheezy old man said. "I've got five grandsons. I know what kids are like. They have dirty sneakers and baggy sweaters and wear their baseball caps back to front."

"That's me." Sam put his cap back on his head. "Honest, Mister. That's me."

"I hate those kids," the old man said angrily. Sam heard the door unlock. "I never liked them from the time that they were born."

The old man opened the door a chink.

As the old man tried to undo the chain, Sam knew this was not a lucky room. He ran swiftly along the corridor and stepped inside the cleaner's closet. It had brooms and rags in it, like in his dream. Through a crack in the closet door he saw a big fat old fellow with a bulgy nose stick his head out of his hotel room. "Ventriloquists!" the old man said. And slammed the door.

Sam waited until he heard the chain on the door, and then came back into the light.

Farther up the hallway he heard the elevator pass. He heard it make a small ringing noise one or two floors below. He knew he should have admitted defeat and gone downstairs in his torn pajamas, but he was not the son of a gambler for nothing. In spite of everything, he believed in luck, the Big Bazoohley. And now he looked at all the numbered doors lined up along the corridor as if they were a deck of cards.

One of these doors would be a *lucky* number. He felt the power in his bones, the power to guess the right number. His arms tingled, his fingers went loose, and he made his eyes go out of focus, just like his father did before he placed a bet at the casino. He walked up the corridor and stopped outside Room 2234.

There were definitely grown-ups in Room 2234.

Their dinner had been delivered on a trolley and when they had finished, they had pushed the trolley out into the corridor. There were two plates of chicken, hardly touched, and a large slab of chocolate cake with a little flag sticking in the cherry on the top.

Sam kicked on the door.

"Just leave it outside," a woman called. It was a young voice, light and breathy.

"Excuse me," Sam said. "I got locked out of my room."

"Please go away," the young man said. "You're not being very thoughtful."

"I'm just a kid."

"He wants a tip," the man said.

"I gave him a tip," the woman said. "He got a good tip when he came. He knows we got the Honeymoon Special Rate. Why can't he just leave us alone?"

"I'm not a waiter," Sam cried.

But then a minute later a crisp new five-dollar bill came sliding out under the door.

If this wasn't luck, what was? He folded the money and tucked it into the pocket of his pajama jacket.

He thought, I'm on a winning streak.

He took the chocolate cake from the trolley and sat down on the floor and began to eat it.

Sam was not a tidy eater. He never had been. And now that he was excited, he had no time to think about the chocolate on his nose and ears. He patted the five dollars under his pajamas with chocolaty hands. He asked himself what his dad would have done. Then he put his eyes out of focus. He made his arms and shoulders go loose. He walked up the corridor, waiting for the next lucky number to speak to him.

SIX

TWO PLUS TWO PLUS TWO plus one equals seven, the luckiest number of all.

Sam stood outside Room 2221, his eyes hooded, his arms loose beside him. He was confident that this was a lucky room. He knocked lightly, barely brushing the wood with his knuckles.

The door swung open so quickly he jumped.

The first thing he saw were the M&M's, a packet of them, in a woman's hand. The woman was short and plump, dressed in a white dressing gown. She had a very small mouth. The eyes behind her spectacles looked red, as if she had been weeping. There was a large lace handkerchief in her hand. When her eyes

2221

rested on Sam, the first thing she did was blow her nose, not loudly, but very sharply.

She tucked her handkerchief in her sleeve and looked at Sam with her head tilted a little to one side. The glass in her spectacles was thick and made her eyes look like little blue fish in an aquarium.

"A boy," she said. She seemed to be speaking to herself, but with a sort of wonder. It was as if she had opened her door and seen a green-backed lizard or a space creature.

"Who is it, Muriel?" a man called.

A small private smile appeared on her face. She slipped the M&M's into her dressing gown pocket. "It's a boy," she said. "With chocolate on his nose and ears."

"I sleepwalked out of my room," Sam said.

"Come on, darling." The woman held out her hand to him. "It's okay. We have a boy, too. He's nine. I bet you're nine."

But Sam did not need to be invited in. "Our boy is sick," the woman whispered. A curly-haired boy was sleeping in the big bed.

Sam looked hard at the man, who had to step back into a closet to let them pass. He was tall and stooped, with a mild, indefinite face. He smiled vaguely at Sam.

Sam began to smile back, but Muriel took him by his shoulders, turned him sharp left, and pushed him into the bathroom.

"A very *grubby* boy," she said quietly, to herself, as she turned on the bath and began unpacking bottles from a little plastic Perfecto case on the countertop.

Sam watched the steaming water rising in the bath.

"Probably," Muriel said, "the grubbiest boy I have ever seen."

"Are you going to give him a bath?" Sam asked.

Muriel turned and looked at him, her eyes wobbling behind her thick lenses. "What?"

"Are you going to give your son a bath?"

"My son is clean, kiddo."

"I sleepwalked out of my room," Sam said. "My parents are probably looking for me."

"Of course they are, but I wouldn't want to see our Wilfred with a filthy face like yours, and I'm sure your parents are no different," she said. "Quick, out of these. Quick, quick." She snapped her fingers and Sam saw that she meant that he should get out of his pajamas and into the bath.

"No," he said. "Sorry."

"Nonsense," Muriel said. She took her pack of

M&M's, found a red one, popped it in her mouth. Then she rolled up the sleeves of her dressing gown and opened a drawstring bag from which she removed a sponge, then a whole series of brushes. "I know how Mommies like to see their little boys."

"I'm sorry," Sam said. "But you're a stranger."

"The kid's right," said the man, who was standing in the doorway. "He doesn't need a bath to wipe his face."

"It isn't just his *face,* George," Muriel said. She began to squeeze a bright red solution onto the bristles of the brush.

Sam knew what that red solution was. He had seen the TV commercial.

"All right," Muriel said. "It's face, arms, hands, and hair. No bath," she said, and she pulled the plug. "But by golly gee, my kiddo, there's work to do on you."

And without more ado she set to work on him. She washed his face, not once, but twice. She scrubbed his arms and scoured his elbows. He called out to tell her to stop it, but she said she knew how Mommies liked their boys to be. She got her plump arm around his neck and scrubbed away. When she had finished with that, she put a fresh hotel towel across his shoulders and she doused his hair with water and poured green Perfecto shampoo on it. She had strong little fingers and she rubbed his head like no one had ever rubbed it in his life. She rinsed the shampoo off with an ice bucket full of water and then shampooed again.

This was not a lucky room. Sam saw that now, but when he had seen the M&M's, he had had this half-crazy idea that they were a magic sign that would lead him to Mr. de Vere. Now the only thing he wanted was to get out of there.

"I just want my mum and dad," he called. He had soap in his eyes, water in his mouth. "Please let me go."

"You'll get your mom and dad," George said. He said this in such a firm way that Sam felt a little surge of hope.

"*Muriel . . .*" George said, his voice rising in a kind of warning.

"Get me the yellow cleanser," Muriel said.

George stepped into the bathroom, looked at all the

bottles and tubes on the countertop, and picked one of them up. He held it out to Muriel.

A boy's voice called, "Who's that?"

"Go to sleep, darling," the woman called back. "It's nothing. George, make sure he stays in his bed."

But the boy had already appeared at the door, his head tucked underneath his father's arm. He had lots of blond curly hair and his face was covered with red spots.

"Who's that?" the boy asked.

"Oh, look at you," Muriel wailed. "Look at my beautiful, beautiful boy." And she began to cry.

She put the soap back on the rack. She put the bristly brush back on the countertop. She let go of Sam Kellow, dried her hands, and took the curly-headed boy away.

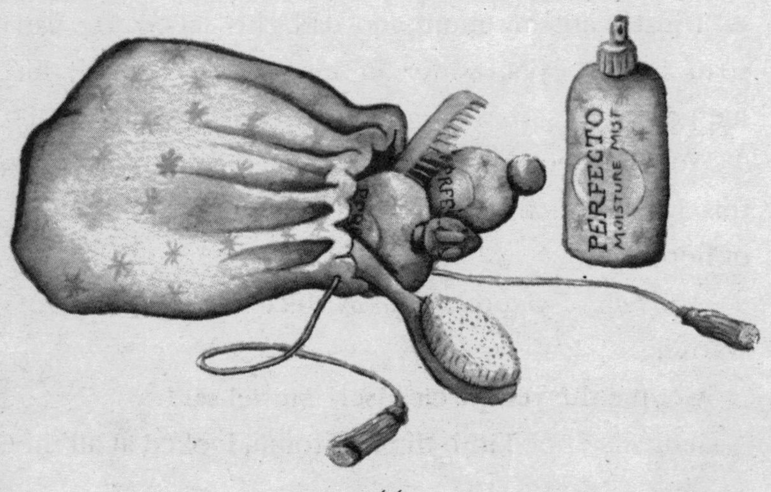

"Just let her finish cleaning you," George said to Sam. "That's all she wants. Once you're nice and clean, then you can go. Believe me," he said, "that's easiest for all of us."

Sam sat down on the toilet seat. "What's your kid's name?" he asked.

"That's Wilfred."

"He's got chicken pox," Sam said. "That's what's making him feel sick."

"We know," George said. "We know very well he has chicken pox." Those mild soap-pale eyes were suddenly blazing with temper. "We don't need grubby little urchins knocking on our door to tell us that."

"I'm just a kid," Sam said. "You don't have to talk to me like that."

"That's right," George said bitterly. "You're an ordinary kid with an ordinary life and ordinary parents. It makes no difference to you if you get chicken pox or not."

Sam was about to say that he had already had chicken pox, but then Muriel came back into the bathroom and started rolling up her sleeves again.

"Muriel," George said. "I really think he's clean now."

"I can't give him back in this state," said Muriel, and she began to take out the brushes again.

"Muriel . . ."

"Don't lecture me," she said. "I can't help myself. I see a filthy boy, I've got to make him nice. It's me. It's who I am. You knew when you married me. You knew when you met me. I'm a mother. I was born to be a mother."

"You wiped my face," the man said. "The first day we met."

"I sponged the mark on your tie."

"Excuse me," Sam said.

"You just wait," Muriel said. "You wait until you're presentable."

"No," said Sam, "I've had enough."

"Just let me get you clean."

"For heaven's sake, Muriel . . ."

"I'll phone his folks," Muriel said, "if that would calm everybody down. I'll phone them so no one needs to worry. What's your name?" she asked Sam. "Sam Kellow? I'll phone them now. George will phone them. He'll tell them you'll be back as soon as you're clean."

While George was out of the room, Muriel stood and looked at Sam. First she was kind of bad-tempered-looking, and then something in her softened. She put her head to one side and squinted her eyes as Sam had sometimes seen his mother do when she was looking at one of her paintings.

"George," she called. Her voice was different, quiet, almost a whisper, as if she did not wish to disturb the beautiful thought that was now suspended in the air in front of her.

"George," she said again, not taking her swimming goldfish eyes off Sam. You could see her creeping up on the thought like a hunter with a net.

"George Bear," she whispered. "Come here to Mama."

In a moment George was back, sticking his long sad nose around the bathroom door.

"Georgey Porgey," said Muriel, gently folding up the wet washcloth. "Georgey Porgey, do you know what I am thinking?"

"You're thinking he should have the chicken pox, not Wilfred."

"Aside from that," said Muriel. She was acting quite differently, shyly even. She lined up all her Perfecto brushes and Perfecto soaps on the countertop in a shy and girlish kind of way.

"You're thinking we just lost the ten thousand dollars."

"I'm thinking," Muriel said, turning to her husband

with her round tight face all red and shiny with excitement, "I'm thinking that our visitor scrubs up quite well."

"You got him nice and clean, it's true."

"I'm thinking," Muriel said slowly, raising her thin black eyebrows, "that the grub is really quite a butterfly."

"True."

"I'm thinking"—a bright red smile stretched across her face—"that the chicken pox needn't stop us from winning the prize."

"What prize?" Sam asked.

"The Perfecto Kiddo Prize." She turned on Sam. "Which we would have won if you hadn't given Wilfred your chicken pox."

For a moment there was total silence in the room. Sam saw George swallow and suck in his cheeks.

"Muriel," said George in a hushed tight voice. "Be fair. . . ."

"I am being fair," snapped Muriel. "I'm thinking that I'm going to give him a chance to make up for what he's done. That's fair. That's very fair. You lost us ten thousand dollars," she said to Sam.

"No I didn't."

"Oh, yes you did, you little grub."

"How?"

"I told you," she said. "You gave him your chicken pox. *Comprende?*"

"Yes," said Sam. What he understood was that Muriel was more than peculiar. She was crazy.

"Good." Muriel smiled. "So now I'm going to let you get it back for us."

But if Muriel now looked more relaxed, George looked more alarmed. "I think, sweetie, that the boy is right. He really should be home in bed."

"But you talked to his parents," said Muriel. "Isn't that so?"

"Y . . . e . . . s," said George.

"No you didn't," Sam said. "You don't even know their names. You couldn't have."

"It's Bellow," piped up Muriel. "You told me."

"Yes, it's Bellow," George said. "You told my wife."

"You told the Bellows," Muriel said, "that their son was safe and sound with us?"

"Oh, Muriel, please . . ." George said.

"You told them we were considering entering him in the competition? You did say that to them, George?"

"Muriel," George said, "you really must be calm."

"I am calm," she said. "I am perfectly calm."

"You can't just steal children."

"For heaven's sake!" she shouted. "I am only *borrowing* the little beast. Until noon tomorrow," she said. "That's all. It is only fair."

The door out of the hotel room was just on the other side of the bathroom door, on the other side of George's spindly legs.

Sam was going to walk out that door the moment he got a chance.

"Fair's fair," he said, and waited for his kidnappers to relax their guard.

SEVEN

WHEN MURIEL WOUND a sheet around Sam's shoulders, he did not even make a face. When she started coating his wet hair with pink sticky goo from a big pot, he stayed so still that Muriel called him "little lamb."

At five past one, the two peculiar grown-ups were winding curlers into his hair, bumping into each other, arguing, pulling his head this way, pushing it the other. He watched them share their pack of M&M's. It was now four hours past his bedtime, but Sam Kellow was wide awake, as cunning as a fox.

In this way he learned that his kidnappers were professionals in the Perfecto Kiddo game. If there was a

contest in Rome or Vienna, they were there, buying the Perfecto products, collecting the coupons, filling out the forms in German or Italian, dressing up their child in grown-up clothing, making all their money from chubby little Wilfred, who had gone back to sleep in his foldaway bed. They were like circus owners with a performing bear, and the bear was their child.

"It's one-thirty and we're only halfway through." George yawned. "We're crazy to do this now. We should do it in the morning."

Sam craned his neck to look at what they'd done to him. But when he caught sight of himself in the big gold-framed mirror, he hardly recognized himself. He looked like a woman who'd gone to the supermarket with her hair in curlers.

"There'll be no time in the morning," Muriel said.

"Muriel, sweetie pie, just relax."

"Relax?" Muriel's face started to go red.

George began to sigh and pat his hands in the air as if this might calm her.

"Relax?" Muriel's voice became a shriek. "If we were both as relaxed as you, we'd still be entering dog food contests.

"Relax!" she muttered and unzipped a big canvas

bag. Out of it she wheeled a big domed-looking thing. It was like a big plastic hat, like a huge egg on a shining metal stand. It was like something you would see in a space movie, for stealing your thoughts or letting you see into the future.

They wheeled this over and fitted it over Sam's head. His skin prickled. His heart thumped. Now, for the first time, he was scared.

Muriel turned on a switch, and a loud roaring noise filled Sam's ears. He nearly panicked. He almost slid out from under and ran. Then he felt the heat and realized the big dome was a hair dryer, the kind his mother sometimes sat under in the beauty salon.

"Relax," he told himself as the hot air circled his head.

Indeed, it was kind of nice inside the hair dryer. For one thing, he could not hear George and Muriel. If he shut his eyes, he did not have to look at his nasty red nose and her goldfish eyes.

Eyes closed, he thought of happy things, things far from here. In his mind he went back to the door marked

CLEANING 201. He opened the door. But this time he walked along a white-tiled passageway. And then he was asleep, lost in a happy dream where his mother and the molelike Mr. de Vere were eating Bombe Alaska at a glass-topped table.

It was the silence that woke him. The hair dryer was turned off. He opened his eyes to feel Muriel lifting the hair dryer off his head. He shut his eyes again, but the dream would not come back. Muriel was removing the curlers from his hair.

"There," she said. "Now, don't you want to see your handsome face?"

Sam opened his eyes as Muriel held up the mirror.

He looked into the glass. Wilfred looked back. Except it was not Wilfred, it was Sam Kellow, and his hair was big and curly like the choirboy in the Perfecto commercial. They had turned him into a Wilfred.

"He's beautiful," Muriel cooed. "The little grub is beautiful!"

Crazy Muriel and Droopy George embraced each other. They did a sort of dance around the room.

"Oh, you're a genius," said George. "You're a genius."

"I am," said Muriel. "I am. I am a total genius."

Sam looked across at Wilfred and saw he was awake.

He was watching his parents dancing around Sam and two big tears ran down his cheeks.

"He's going to win my money," he said. "That's what's happening. He's going to win my money."

It was then, while watching the tears course down Wilfred's spotty face, that Sam saw he did not need to find Mr. de Vere.

One door had shut, but another had opened. His dad had been right. Sam had found what he had been looking for: the power to win ten thousand dollars. The Big Bazoohley.

EIGHT

THE TWO BOYS LOOKED so much alike it was scary. True, Sam had Sonic the Hedgehog on his pajamas, and Wilfred's pajamas were a cream-colored sort of flannel, but when George and Muriel tucked the two boys up together into the grown-up bed, you could not see the pajamas, just these two twin faces.

They were not perfect twins, of course. Wilfred's nose was a little broader than Sam's. Wilfred had spots, Sam did not. Wilfred was asleep, and Sam was lying under the covers, wide awake, thinking about the Big Bazoohley.

Of course, Droopy George and Nasty Muriel planned

to keep the prize money for themselves, but he figured he would deal with that when the time came. Now all he thought of was the good part.

If he had ten thousand dollars, he could take that scary look off his father's face. He could pay the bill for the hotel room. He could hire a private detective to find Mr. de Vere. If he had ten thousand dollars, he could take his mum and dad to a funny movie and make them laugh again.

Soon he was lying on his back, happily snoring.

It seemed like only a moment later he heard Wilfred say, "Mommy, what are you doing to my clothes?"

"Be quiet," Muriel said.

Sam opened his eyes and saw that the curtains were open and it was morning. Great fat flakes of snow were swirling in the sky outside. Muriel was sitting on the end of the bed, snipping with her scissors. George was asleep sitting up in a straight-backed chair.

"You're cutting my velvet suit," Wilfred whined.

"I am not *cutting* it," Muriel said. "And do not scratch or you'll get scars on your face and look ugly forever."

But Sam could see that Wilfred was not scratching. He had just woken up and was rubbing his eyes.

"You're cutting my velvet *suit,*" he said to his mother.

"I am not," she said.

But she was. She had a big pair of scissors and was going *snip snip snip*.

"You are."

"Do you want to *wake* him?" Muriel said. "Why do you think your parents have spent the night sleeping in straight-backed chairs? We want him to sleep. We don't want him to go in the competition with circles under his eyes."

"I want a baseball cap like his," Wilfred said. "And one of those sweaters with the numbers on the back."

"Don't be ridiculous," his mother said. "What sort of idiot goes to bed in a baseball cap?"

"I wouldn't sleep in it," Wilfred cried. "I'd never wear it to bed. I'd just wear it when I was outside."

Muriel looked up from her sewing and Sam saw something in her soften.

"I'm sorry, my darling," she said, "you're just not that sort of boy. I'm sorry I have to hurt your lovely clothes, but we need this little grub to win the prize. No one will know it isn't you. He'll have your name. I have to alter your clothes so they will fit him."

"Then I can have his baseball cap."

"You can't have my baseball cap," Sam said, sitting up

in bed. “And no one,” he said to Muriel, “can call me Wilfred. I’m Sam. Sam Kellow.”

“You’ll do what you’re told,” said George, stretching his long, stiff, storky legs. His face looked blotchy and pasty, and he needed a shave. He stood and rubbed his eyes and went to stare down at the snowbound city.

“Come and look at this, Wilfred!” he called. “It’s pretty as a postcard.”

George and Wilfred now had their backs to him at the window. Muriel had her head down over her scissors. Sam could have run right out the door, right there and then.

Instead he yawned and snuggled back under the covers. What he had in mind was a nice nap, and then ten thousand dollars just in time for lunch.

But this, it seemed, was not to be.

“Wakey, wakey,” Muriel said briskly. And pulled the covers off.

“But you said the competition wasn’t until twelve.”

“There’s lots to do before twelve,” said George. “First we have to teach you table manners à la Perfecto.”

NINE

"SIT UP STRAIGHT,"
said George.

"Use your fork," said Muriel.

"Do you want to end up with peas on the floor?" hollered George. "Do you know what happens if you have peas on the floor? Every pea," he said, "they subtract fifteen points."

"Do you have any idea," Muriel said, "what five little green peas could mean?"

"Seventy-five points," said Sam, quick as a flash, although there was not a pea in sight and he was sitting with an empty white plate in front of him. "Five times fifteen equals seventy-five."

"This is not a math contest," said Muriel nastily. "If you dropped five peas in front of the judges, you would have no hope of being Perfecto Kiddo. It wouldn't matter how perfecto your hair was. Not even Wilfred's hair could save you. You would be a disgrace, and I would be so angry with you, I don't know what I'd do."

"You'd pull his nose," Wilfred said.

Sam looked up from the little table George had set up for him to practice at. He wished he was Wilfred. Wilfred was lying on the king-size bed with Sam's baseball cap perched on top of his shining, curly head.

"Actually," said Muriel, "I think I'd twist his ear."

"But Mom . . ." Wilfred said. "He's *trying*. He's *trying* really hard."

When Wilfred said that, Sam stopped being mad with him about the baseball cap (although he wished *he* was wearing the baseball cap himself and not this nerdy velvet suit and this ridiculous bow tie).

"Now we have to practice for the spaghetti test," said Muriel. "Chop, chop, come along. We can't leave anything to chance."

"He can't practice for spaghetti without real spaghetti," said George.

"Sweetie bear," said Muriel, smiling through

clenched teeth, "he can't eat spaghetti now. If he eats real spaghetti now, he'll ruin his appetite for the competition. Don't you remember what happened in Madrid?"

"That, my precious pretty footsie," said George, who was starting to go a little red above his collar, "that is what I mean. How can we have him practice his spaghetti-eating without real spaghetti? Nothing is as slimy as real spaghetti. Nothing is quite as splattery as real spaghetti sauce."

"Maybe they won't have spaghetti," Wilfred said. "Maybe they'll have tough steak instead."

"They had spaghetti in Tokyo," said Muriel. "And in Paris. Oh, you were so good in Paris, Wilfred. It was your most perfecto win. Remember, George, how they had the four-foot-long spaghetti strands? Those horrid judges. Those horrid, horrid French judges. But Wilfred wound that long, long strand on his fork, and not a drop, not a drop did he spill."

"My mum cuts up my spaghetti for me," said Sam.

"Your 'mum' will be nowhere near you," said George, "and I am going to teach you how to eat spaghetti like an adult."

"How?"

"With string," said George, slipping an M&M into his mouth, "and soap."

"Not to eat," said Wilfred. "He doesn't mean eat. He means wind it around your fork."

Five minutes later Sam was sitting at the table with a sheet wound around him. In front of him was a bowl of slimy tangled soapy string. As Sam looked on, George unscrewed the cap off a bottle of blue ink and poured it over the top.

"Not a splatter," he said. "Not a drop."

"I can't do that," Sam said. "I know I can't."

"Oh, yes you can," said George, taking a fork in his long bony fingers. "Now watch me, laddie, watch me closely."

Sam watched him. It was not a pleasant sight.

TEN

THEY PRACTICED THE spaghetti and (because they wished to take no chances) they practiced holding elbows against your side when you cut tough steak, and just when Sam thought it would go on forever, George and Muriel declared themselves done.

"Now it is quiet time," Muriel said. "It's nine o'clock and we have to present ourselves to the judges and do the paperwork."

"We'll take him with us," George said. "I'm not letting him bolt at this stage."

"No, George," said Muriel. "I really don't think we

can afford to take the risk. I don't want them looking at Wilfred's photograph and— "

"Comparisons are invidious," sniffed George.

"Precisely," said Muriel.

"What's invidious?" asked Wilfred.

"It's what will happen to you if you let him escape."

"Oh, I'll be here," said Sam, "but don't you think it would be sensible if you let me write a note to my mum and dad so they wouldn't worry?"

"If they're going to worry, they're worried already."

"Oh, no," Sam said. "It's a Saturday. They won't wake up until ten."

"Really?" Muriel wrinkled her nose and her eyes swam in amazement. "How extraordinary. What peculiar people they must be."

"I think my note should say that I'll be back after the competition," Sam said. "You wouldn't want them worrying or calling the police or anything."

Sam could see this subject had also been on George's mind because he now cocked his head and looked at Sam with great interest.

"Go on," he said, eating one M&M after another. "Go on."

"Well," said Sam, "it's no big deal. I just thought I'd

write a note and say I was okay and that I'd be back—"

"For a late lunch," said George. He held out the pack of M&M's to Sam for the first time. "For a late lunch," he said. "This is excellent." This is exactly what we should do. We'll be on the road by one, one-thirty at the latest."

Muriel looked at George. She gave him a long, long look that suggested she was somehow very disappointed in him for being so easily persuaded. But then she fetched some paper with the hotel's name printed in gold letters and placed it on the table where Sam had been practicing.

"Give him your pen," she said to George.

George hesitated, as if his pen were a toy he didn't want to share.

"Give him your pen, honey bear," said Muriel.

George took a very expensive-looking black-and-gold pen from his pocket, removed its cap, and handed it carefully to Sam, who immediately began to write with it. It was a peculiar pen with a hard steel nib and it was not easy to write with, but after two bad starts and two new sheets of paper, he succeeded in writing this message:

KING REDWARD HOTEL

Dear Mum and Dad,
had to slip out for a
moment. I've gone to
get the Big Bazoohley.
I'll be back for a
late lunch.

George took back his pen and looked carefully at the nib. Then he screwed the top back on and put the pen in his pocket. Then he picked up the letter Sam had written and blew on the ink to dry it.

"Big Bazoohley?" said George. "Bazoohley?"

"It's a hide-and-seek game," Sam said quickly, "that we play at home."

George narrowed his watery blue eyes and knelt down so his red pointy nose was level with Sam's. "The Big Bazoohley?" he said. He had been drinking last night and his breath did not smell nice. "If it's hide-and-seek, how could you come *home* with it? If it was hide-and-seek, you would come home *after* playing it. But you"—he picked up the paper and peered at it closely—"you wrote, 'I've gone to get the Big Bazoohley.' "

"Oh, for heaven's sake," said Muriel, "this is no time to argue about grammar."

"Darling," said George, and his long neck was now excessively red. "This is not grammar I am arguing about."

"You always say that," she said, "but it always is. If you make a joke, it is about grammar. If I see you smile, it is because I made a mistake with my grammar. Now, please, you go and put this letter under their door."

"It's number 2235," said Sam.

"You put this under the door at Room 2235," Muriel said, "while I have a little chat with our guest."

As George left the room, Muriel turned to Sam and took his hand. She held it lightly and stroked the back of it. "If you run away, my sweetie," she said, "if you play this Big Bazoohley with me, you will find you are dealing with a Big Bazoohley expert. Because I'll come after you. And I will find you, wherever you are hiding. And I will take you by the ear and I will pull you back and make you eat soap and string with ink on it. Do you believe me?"

Sam looked into Muriel's wild swimming eyes. "Yes," he said.

"And do you know how I would find you?"

"No," said Sam.

"By smell," said Muriel. "Because I am a witch, I am a real-life witch. Do you believe me?"

"Yes," said Sam.

"All right," said Muriel, and then she actually kissed him on the cheek. "Then you stay put, and everything will be just fine."

And with that she picked up her purse and walked briskly out of the room.

"Of course," said Wilfred, when the door shut behind her, "she's not a witch."

"I knew that," Sam said.

"But she can get kind of scary, too," Wilfred said. "Even when she worked as a checkout clerk at Woolworth, people were scared of her. There'd be long lines at the other checkouts, and she'd be just standing there waiting for someone to check out with her. I was only four, but I used to watch how people stayed away from her."

Sam felt sorry for Wilfred. He thought how terrible it must be to have such a scary mum.

"She's not so bad," said Wilfred, who seemed to guess what Sam was thinking. "I just wish she'd let me wear a baseball cap."

"All kids wear baseball caps," said Sam, "even in Australia, where I'm from. We play cricket, but we wear baseball caps. If you go to Sydney, you'll see kids with caps from Boston, New York, Philadelphia— "

"But I'm *from* Philadelphia," Wilfred said. "I'm an American."

"What's that got to do with it?"

"It's our game," Wilfred said. "I'm American. I'm *entitled* to the cap."

"Do you know who the Toronto Blue Jays are?" Sam said.

"Do *you* know?" Wilfred sniffed. "That's more the point. You're the Australian, not me."

Sam ignored this. "They sell Blue Jays caps downstairs," he said. "There's a little shop."

Wilfred's eyes got a sad faraway look. "I know," he said. "I saw them. If we were here in summer, we could see them play at the SkyDome. Except," he said sadly, "you could, but I couldn't."

"But you could have the cap," Sam said.

"Might as well be on the moon," Wilfred said. "They'd never buy me one."

"But I've got money," Sam said.

And he went to the bathroom, where his pajamas were neatly folded just where Muriel had placed them. His five-dollar tip was still in the pocket. He brought it back and showed it to Wilfred.

"Wow," said Wilfred. He took the money and held it for a moment. Then he passed it back to Sam.

"No," Sam said, giving the bill back to him. "This," said Earl Kellow's son, "is for you to buy your Blue Jays hat."

For a moment he thought Wilfred was going to cry.

"You'd buy me a baseball hat? Why would you do that?"

"Because they're not being fair to you. Why do they eat M&M's all the time and never offer any to you?"

"They're being much less fair to you," Wilfred said. "They're being total jerks."

"Oh, that's okay," Sam said.

For a moment Wilfred's eyes looked like his father's, emotional and suspicious. "This is a trick," he said. "You'll give me the money and when I leave the room, you'll run away."

"I could have run away a hundred times. I could run away right now if I wanted."

"Cross your heart you won't run away."

"Ridgey-didge."

"Is that like Big Bazoohley?"

"Ridgey-didge. It's Australian. It means 'honest.' It means 'I swear it.' "

"What if they see me?"

"Cross your fingers," Sam said.

Wilfred crossed the fingers of his right hand. Sam put the five-dollar bill in his left.

"But I've got chicken pox. I've got spots all over my face."

"Here," said Sam. "Take my cap and pull it down over your face."

Wilfred put the hat on and pulled it down.

"Do I look okay?"

But Sam was already relaxing on the bed doing his favorite hotel thing: watching an NBA game on cable TV.

ELEVEN

WILFRED HAD THE shining new Blue Jays cap perched on top of his head when Muriel came into the room. He should have been caught, but his mother was so excited about the Big Bazoohley, she did not look at anyone but Sam. She came into the room with a Perfecto hairbrush in her hand, ready for action, and by the time she actually looked at Wilfred, he had hidden the baseball cap under his pillow. There was now only half an hour to go and even Sam was getting excited, though not half as excited as

George and Muriel. They combed and brushed. They sprayed. They sponged and patted. They kneeled at his feet, pulling and tugging at his suit, putting a pin here, removing a little lint there.

"When you walk into the ballroom," Muriel called up to him, "you will see there are a lot of tables with white cloths. That is where you will eat, but you must not sit there."

"That's not the right way to tell the boy," said George, unscrewing a bottle of shoe polish and applying it with a tissue.

"Oh no, my dearest? And how should I tell him?"

"What you must do, young fellow," George said, speaking carefully as he applied more polish to Sam's left shoe, "what you must do is walk to the line of chairs on the wall at your left."

Looking down, Sam saw him fold a yellow cloth and then begin to buff his left shoe furiously.

"You will already be being judged," George puffed. "They will be looking at your hair. They will watch how it catches the light, how it moves, how it shines. But as the commercial says—you've seen the commercials?—'Perfecto isn't just about hair.' They'll be judging your clothes, the way you walk, the way you sit. To sit in someone else's chair would lose you ten points. Can you remember that? Tell me the number."

"Thirty-two." They had told him that last night. Sam never forgot a number.

"There," said George, smiling up at Muriel. "He knows now."

"He knows nothing," said Muriel.

She stood slowly, glowering at Sam from behind her weird thick glasses. "Who is Mr. Lopate?" she asked.

Sam shrugged.

"You *see.*" Muriel looked down at George, who was carefully packing up his shoe polish and cloth in a shoe box. "He's a foreigner. He knows nothing. He knows totally nothing. First you will absolutely not touch your hair, ever, no matter. Do you understand that?"

"Yes."

"Even if it itches."

"Yes."

"Sometimes the shampoo might make your head a little itchy. If you scratch, you are out."

"What about Mr. Lopate?" Sam asked.

"He is a very famous movie star. I can't believe he isn't famous in whatever horrid little place you come from. You will see him in front of you the moment you take your seat. He will be seated at the podium. Do you know what a podium is?"

"It's a sort of platform."

"Correct. On this 'sort of platform' you will see a remarkably handsome gentleman sitting on a chair. That is Phillip Lopate, and all that matters in your little life is that Phillip Lopate likes you."

"Seat thirty-two is right in front of Mr. Lopate's nose." George stood, holding his box of shoe polish. "It is a very good number. He cannot miss you."

"You will have a *blue* number thirty-two. And when you stand to dance," Muriel said, "you will go to the little girl who will have a *pink* thirty-two. Her name is Nancy See and she has particularly good hair. She dances nicely, too, which is why all the old hands are so jealous of her. She's new to the competition circuit, but everyone thinks she's going to win."

"You never said anything about dancing," Sam said.

"Well," said Muriel, "I am saying it now." And they both began to laugh.

"I can't dance," Sam said.

There was sudden absolute silence in the room. Everybody was staring at Sam.

"You fox-trot at least," Muriel said at last. "That's all

that's needed. You can get by on fox-trot. That horrid little blond boy who won in Tokyo—that's really all he could do, the fox-trot."

But Sam had never even heard of a dance called the fox-trot, and he could see the Big Bazoohley slipping out of his grasp. "I can't dance the fox-trot," he said quietly. "I just can't dance."

"Oh, heavens," said Muriel. And she sat on the bed with her head in her hands. "Oh, Lord help us."

Wilfred slipped off the bed. "I'll teach you," he said. "It isn't hard."

"How can you teach anyone to dance in half an hour?" wailed Muriel.

"I'm a fast learner," said Sam.

But Muriel started yelling at him: "You tricked me! You tricked me into this— "

"Muriel!" said George. "Relax!"

"Relax!" she shrieked, leaping off the bed so high she seemed to fly. "I did all this work. I've added body and bounce to his filthy hair. He never told me he couldn't dance. I pinned my hopes on him. I bribed that stupid man so he would give him seat thirty-two."

"No one told me I had to dance," Sam said.

"How could it be a Perfecto Kiddo Prize if you couldn't dance?"

"Chop, chop," said George. "It's not too late to learn. Come on, Wilfred, you'll have to be the girl. Okay now, I'm the orchestra."

And, still seated in his straight-backed chair, the strange stooped man in the cardigan began to wave his arms around and thump his foot and croon in a strange high voice.

TWELVE

SAM WALKED INTO THE elevator in front of George and Muriel. He was their dancing bear. He had a blister on his heel from trying to fox-trot in Wilfred's shining shoes.

"Don't limp," hissed George as he pressed the button for the lobby. "The Perfecto Kiddo never limps."

Sam was about to explain about the blister, when out in the hallway a man's voice called, "Hold that lift."

Straightaway George's long white finger darted out. He did not press the OPEN DOOR button. He pressed CLOSE DOOR and the elevator doors began to slide shut. But before they could close completely, a large square hand hooked around one of them, and then a tall man

pushed his shoulder in between the doors and forced them back open.

And there, in the elevator doorway, stood Sam's dad.

Earl Kellow had such a worried face, Sam hardly recognized him. He was normally such a big man, such a smiling man. But now, as he pushed his way into the elevator, he was kind of shrunken and stooped over and even Sam's mother—who was only a second behind him—was huddled inside her parka, her arms crossed tight across her chest, her eyes red, her hair untidy.

Sam felt terrible to cause his parents so much pain, but he also knew straightaway that if they saw him, he could never have a chance to get the money. So he hunched over, too. He pushed his hands into his pockets and looked down at the floor so no one could see his face.

"Stand up," said George. "You'll never win if you hunch."

Muriel turned to him.

"What does it matter," she said bitterly. "He can't dance worth a whistle. He doesn't have a chance."

The elevator car was smaller than Sam's bathroom at home. There was no way to hide from anyone. Sam stood up straight and looked straight ahead.

His mother was looking up at the lighted numbers as the elevator descended, but Earl Kellow's eyes were looking around the car. Sam felt his father's eyes pass over him. It was only then Sam realized how much he had changed since his parents tucked him into bed the night before and kissed him good night. His baseball cap was gone. His long straight hair was gone. He now had curly hair. He had a velvet suit and a bow tie. He had clean, manicured nails. He had scrubbed and polished skin.

It was like being invisible. It was the weirdest, most confusing feeling. One part of him felt powerful, the other part really lonely.

His parents looked so sad. He wanted to hug them and tell them that he wasn't lost, that he was on a winning streak, that he was going to win the Big Bazoohley even if he couldn't dance very well. He was going to hire a private detective. He was going to find Mr. de Vere. Everyone was going to be happy again.

But of course he couldn't say a word. He had to stay with Mad Muriel and Droopy George.

"There must be a casino in the hotel," his mother said quietly. "That must be what he meant." The look she gave her husband was full of blame, as if it was his fault that his son was hanging around casinos.

"There are no casinos in Toronto," his father said.

But Sam could see that his mother was so worried she would not believe him. She turned to the strange woman with the red spectacles and dancing blue eyes. "Excuse me," she said to Muriel, "do you know if there's a casino in this hotel?"

"No," Muriel said huffily, "certainly not."

"If you want to throw your money away," George sniffed, "you've got to go across the border."

Sam's mother turned away from Muriel and spoke to her husband in a lower voice. "Perhaps," she said, "he went back on the subway. I think he's trying to find Mr. de Vere."

"No, no," his father said. "He's a good kid."

"He is a *smart* kid," his mother said. "When he says he's getting the Big Bazoohley, he can only mean Mr. de Vere. Earl, he's gone to find Mr. de Vere."

When she said *Bazoohley,* Sam felt George and Muriel go rigid. They held their hands by their sides. They looked up at the lighted numbers. They held their breath. They knew they were in the car with Sam's parents. And when the car arrived in the lobby, they took Sam, one on each side, and marched him, fast, toward the ballroom.

"What does it mean?" George hissed.

"What?" said Sam, as if he did not know.

" 'Bazoohley'," Muriel said. "What does it mean?"

But there was no time for Sam to answer. They were at the registration desk outside the ballroom.

THIRTEEN

YEARS LATER, WHEN THE adventure was all over, Vanessa Kellow painted *Toronto in a Matchbox,* the masterpiece that made her famous.

This painting fit inside a standard-size matchbox and it showed the city of Toronto as it looked on the day that Sam went missing.

It showed the entire city covered with six feet of deep dry-powder snow. It was snow so deep that even the skyscrapers had soft white hats; snow so deep that the Gardiner Expressway closed down, and men and women traveled in from the airport on cross-country skis.

If you look for the corner of Yonge and King Streets

in the painting, you will find the beautiful new King Redward Hotel, and if you take a powerful magnifying glass and peer into that line of lighted yellow windows on the second floor, you will find yourself, miraculously, looking at another, even smaller, painting of the great ballroom.

In this delicate perfect world, you will see the Perfecto Kiddo banners. You will see the three great crystal chandeliers. You will see an upper gallery in which people have crowded to look down at the spectacle below. In this gallery you might recognize Muriel and George, and in the ballroom below you should be able to find the small figure of Sam Kellow walking to take his place at the beginning of the Perfecto Kiddo Competition.

It is a wonderful painting, and justly famous, but it cannot tell you that Sam Kellow's borrowed shoes were pinching his feet, or let you hear the loud noise they made as he walked across the shining floor in front of the judges.

It is really far too small a painting to show you the expression on his face. It cannot tell you that his nose tickled. Or that his head itched. Or that he imagined Mr. Lopate hated him.

When Sam walked across the grand ballroom of the Redward Hotel, he felt as if he had walked into a dream.

In the middle of the room was a sort of raised island on which the judges sat. There were three of them: a young man in a navy-blue suit, a middle-aged woman with a lot of gold jewelry, and a slightly disheveled old man with a handsome face, striking white hair, and rather mild blue eyes. This was Mr. Lopate and people always described those eyes as "kindly," but when Sam saw those eyes watching him, he thought that the chief judge hated him.

On his left he saw the line of chairs George had told him would be there. He quickly found his seat: Number thirty-two was right in the middle of the row.

He sat down. Wilfred's suit was tight under his arms and across his stomach. He undid the buttons of the jacket and put his hands under the belt, trying to stretch it a little looser.

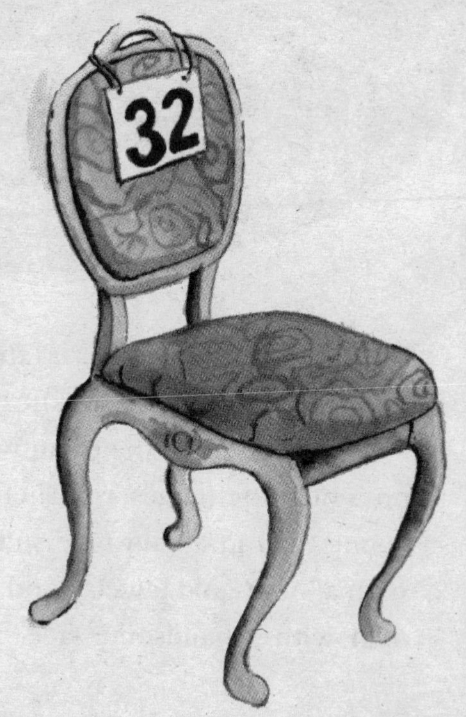

George and Muriel were above the ballroom, on the very edge of the gallery, but even from that distance, they could not leave him alone. They waved and signaled for him to get his hands out of his trousers and do up the buttons of his jacket.

Sam thought they looked idiotic. Just the same, he took his hands out of his trousers and he did do up his buttons. Then he saw Judge Lopate observing him. The judge's lip seemed to curl as he wrote on his scorecard.

He had that leaden feeling he got in his stomach before piano lessons. In a minute, he would have to dance.

Soon the other boy contestants came to sit beside him. These were the rich-looking kids he had seen in the hotel lobby—the redheaded twins in the brown velvet suits, the tall pale boy in the black tuxedo. They were scented like shampoo. They looked happy and as handsome as movie stars.

"Attention, please." It was the youngest of the judges, the man in the navy-blue suit. "The first section of the contest will now commence."

All the boys beside him stood up, so Sam stood, too. He looked up and down the line. There were tall boys and short boys, chubby boys and boys with legs like rake handles, but they all stood up and walked across the floor, as confident as kings, or ambassadors, or senators. They walked toward the girls, who remained seated on the other side of the ballroom.

Some of the girls were tall and some short, and some

thin and some plump, and their hair was of different colors, but they had one thing in common: They all looked very glamorous and sophisticated.

There were strapless ball gowns made of organza, tight sheaths covered with shining sequins, dance dresses shaped like big Icelandic poppies.

Sam walked toward his opposite number—thirty-two. He felt clumsy and stupid in Wilfred's tight suit.

There she was, holding up the number thirty-two. This was the very same girl who had smiled at him in the lobby. She had been wearing a tiara then. He had been plain Sam Kellow with his pathetic little bag of bread and peanut butter. Now she smiled at him again and showed a pretty dimple in her cheek. Sam liked her deep-blue dress, but this only made him feel sadder.

In a moment, he knew, this tall slender girl with the huge excited brown eyes was going to hate him. He knew he was about to step on her shining black shoes.

Then the orchestra began to play. All the boys around him swung their partners onto the floor. There was nothing for him to do but follow their example.

It had been easier dancing with Wilfred. It had been easier following the beat of George's thumping foot. Here in the ballroom, the saxophones got in the way and Sam got lost in the music and stepped on his partner's foot almost as soon as they started. When he saw her wince, he thought he could not continue.

"Look . . ." he began miserably.

"Just move," she said. "Don't be so tense."

He danced one more step and watched her face grimace again. He was embarrassed, humiliated.

"Maybe you can get another partner," he said.

"Come on, dance. Keep moving." Her forehead was creased into a frown. "What are you doing here?" she said. "You don't belong here. How did you get in?"

"It's not my fault," Sam said, dragging his feet after her. From the corner of his eye he could see Mr. Lopate pointing him out to the other judges. "I was kidnapped."

She did not believe him. He could tell.

"I sleepwalked out of my room," he insisted. "And the door locked behind me and my parents couldn't hear me knocking and these creeps grabbed me and put me in this stupid suit. That's kidnapping," he said. "That's what kidnapping is."

"The suit certainly doesn't fit you," she said doubtfully.

"Their son has chicken pox. It's his suit and it's really uncomfortable. I can hardly breathe. If I could breathe," he said apologetically, "I could dance better."

"Where are they—these 'kidnappers'?"

"See, up there, with the red glasses and the droopy fellow with the long nose."

The girl laughed so loudly, she put her hand over her mouth to stop herself.

"Oh," she said, "that's just perfect."

"What? What?"

"That's Wilfred's parents."

"Yes, Wilfred's parents."

"Did they really kidnap you? Did they really? I believe it. I totally believe it. Some of these Perfecto parents are a little strange, but George and Muriel are total fanatics. If they really kidnapped you, you could have them arrested. Everyone would be very happy."

"You *know* them?"

"Well, I'm new. I don't know anyone really well. But even I know about Muriel and George. I don't know how they do it, but Wilfred always wins the boys' prize."

"Well, I want to be perfecto," Sam said. "I want to win this time."

She smiled. "I thought you wanted me to get another partner."

"I have to win. I need the money. And you needn't

laugh," Sam said. "You don't know me. You don't know what I can do."

She *had* been laughing, but now her expression became more sympathetic. "Tell me all about being kidnapped. Was it exciting?"

"I guess it wasn't really kidnapped. I could have run away if I hadn't wanted to win this prize so much," he said mournfully. "They didn't tell me I'd have to dance."

"Actually," the girl said, "you are dancing! Do you realize you're moving to the beat? Not very well," she

said quickly, "but still, you're almost promising. And you do have quite nice hair. The hair is at least half the points."

When the music stopped, he looked across at the judges. Mr. Lopate was still staring at him.

"He can't believe you." The girl giggled. "He thinks you're from the planet Mars."

Sam was hurt by this, but tried not to show it.

"I'm going to win that prize," he said.

"Ladies and gentlemen," the chief judge announced. "Please escort your partners to the allocated tables."

"Come on," the girl said softly. She put out her arm. "It's spag and nag time."

And they walked together to the fifteen tables, which you can see in *Toronto in a Matchbox.* These are round tables, at the right-hand side of the ballroom. Behind the tables, next to the kitchen door, you can see a grinning chef, holding a huge bowl. The bowl is gleaming white and rimmed with gold. Inside you can see, painted in the most meticulous detail, the meal that has the power to change Sam Kellow's life.

FOURTEEN

THE BIG ROUND TABLE was set for eight. "Now," Sam's partner said as they approached it, "when we get to the table, hold the chair out for me. Then as I sit down, push the chair in."

"Okay," Sam said. He did not ask what spag and nag was. He had a nasty feeling he already knew.

"They're not bad kids," she whispered, nodding to the other kids who were already sitting at the table. "I'm Nancy," she said, more loudly.

"Sam," he said.

"That's a nice name," she said.

"Yes," said a tall pale boy in a dinner suit. Sam recognized him from the lobby, too. He had striking, shining jet-black hair down to his shoulders, and an expensive watch shining on his wrist. "Yes," he said. "Sam Peanut Butter, am I right? You eat peanut butter sandwiches so you don't have to pay for room service."

"What's your problem?" Sam said.

"No, no, Geoffrey," said the girl next to him. She had piles of curly strawberry-blond hair and bright, bright blue eyes. "Don't upset him. I've seen him on the dance floor. He's really *violent.*"

"Shut up, Gloria," said Nancy.

The boy with the long jet-black hair covered his mouth with his hand. "Judges can lip-read," he said.

And the girl with the strawberry-blond hair smiled at Nancy as if she was her favorite friend. "Oh dear, Nancy," she said. "I do hope your feet are feeling quite recovered." She picked up her napkin and held it delicately over her mouth. "If he's a clodhopper," she said into her napkin, "he's sure to be a sauce-splatterer. They've put me next to a violent splatterer for spag and nag."

A boy's voice hissed: "Judge incoming."

Then Gloria changed completely. She lowered her napkin and revealed a sweet friendly face.

"I was wondering, Sam," she said, "did we meet in

New York City? Were you staying at the Royalton? I thought I met you with your folks in the lobby."

If Sam had not already seen how creepy she was, he would have thought she was a blond-haired angel.

"Or maybe at JO JO's," she said. "Do you eat at JO JO's? Do you know it? Sixty-fourth and Lex? Or the Metropolitan Club Christmas party."

Of course she was making polite conversation for the judge who was circling the table with a clipboard. Sam knew he would be wise to do the same, but he was so angry about her two-faced act, he did not answer.

"You're supposed to talk, Mr. Peanut Butter," she said when the judge had walked on. "There are a whole six points for conversation. And your hair is horrible, like an old janitor's mop."

"I was never at the Royalton Hotel."

"Neither was I, Monsieur Peanut," said the boy with long black hair. "You're supposed to pretend. And don't glower and glare at me, that won't help you pay for room service."

"Talk to *me,* Sam," Nancy said. "I think your hair is gorgeous."

"Yes, talk to her," said the girl who looked like a porcelain angel. "Not to me, I beg of you."

"Here they come," said the tall boy with the jet-black hair.

Sam expected more judges, but this time it was waiters who came swooping down on the table like great penguins. They left huge plates of salad in front of every Perfecto Kiddo, then retreated.

Sam smelled the salad before he even saw it: the onion, the vinegar in the dressing.

"Eat it," Nancy said. "Pretend you like it. I hate the onions." She smiled at him and began to eat. "I hate the pickles, too," she said. "But when I'm the Perfecto Girl, I'm taking my family to Jamaica and then I'm retiring. I'm thinking about Jamaica."

It was like a dream, but there was no hallway to wake up in. There was no escape from the onions and the pickles. There was nothing to do but eat them. Every time Sam thought he couldn't take another bite, there was Nancy smiling at him. He thought he'd like to take his mum and dad to Jamaica at the same time. He remembered to hold his elbows in. He remembered to use his napkin. He even made some jokes that Nancy thought were funny.

He ate everything on his plate, and the waiters, descending on the table, whisked the empty plates away, refilled the water glasses, and retreated so the judges could come in and circle the table one more time.

So far, so good. Sam knew he had not been a perfect dancer, but he was an optimist and he knew he was having a great conversation with Nancy about Jamaica. He knew it was a great conversation because he wasn't thinking about it until Nancy stopped him.

"Uh-oh," she said. "Here comes the dreaded spag."

The waiters swooped in with big plates of spaghetti and meat sauce. As Sam turned to thank the waiter, he caught sight of Muriel and George up in the gallery. George was looking at him with a little brass telescope. Muriel had a tiny pair of binoculars. Wilfred was not with them. He was locked up in their room, looking at his spotted face and his Blue Jays cap in the bathroom mirror.

Sam put his fork into the spaghetti just the way he had practiced with the slimy string. He used a spoon and a fork. He held the spoon underneath and twirled with the fork on top, and it worked.

"Eureka!" he said to Nancy.

"Man's a pro," said Nancy.

Sam saw the spaghetti twirling onto the fork and he was, for a full ten seconds, a champion, a winner, excited, pleased. He really did have a chance of winning. The spaghetti, he thought, was just like the string he had practiced with.

But string is string and spaghetti is spaghetti and this spaghetti was long, and really slippery, and much more rubbery than string. As Sam lifted it to his mouth, it unwound like a spring.

It did more than simply unwind. It became an elastic band, a catapult. It sent a single gob of sauce flying across the table and, as chance would have it, it landed on the obnoxious tall boy with the jet-black hair. It landed smack on the front of his perfect white dress shirt.

The boy looked at him and shuddered. "You vile little peanut," he said.

"I'm sorry," Sam said. "It was an accident."

He looked up at the judges' podium. He saw Mr. Lopate looking right at him with a weird kind of look in his old face.

"You're dead, Mr. Peanut," the boy said, mopping at his shirtfront with his table napkin. "Why don't you leave the table now and stop ruining it for your betters."

Sam did not like being talked to like this, but on the other hand, the last thing he wanted to do was splatter sauce on Nancy's dress. He wanted her to have her holiday in Jamaica.

"I'm sorry," he said to Nancy, and began to stand.

"No," Nancy said.

But it was too late. He stood at the moment when the waiter was pouring water into his glass and now a whole jugful came spilling down, over his carefully arranged Perfecto hair, over his scrubbed Perfecto face, over Wilfred's suit, and worst of all, it spilled right over Nancy. Her shining hair hung like rattails over her dripping face. She looked like she had fallen into a swimming pool. She had water in her eyes. She was spluttering.

Everyone in the ballroom was looking at them.

He wanted to die. He wished the ballroom floor would open up and swallow him. But when he saw the boy with the jet-black hair laughing behind his napkin, he got mad.

"Get a life," he said, and this time he did not care who heard him.

Sam picked up his fork and dug it deep into his spaghetti. He watched the boy's face change as he stood.

"No . . ." the boy said.

But Sam was already lifting the dripping mess high. And then Sam Kellow flicked.

"Oooooh," said a woman in the gallery.

"Aghh," said the judge with the gold jewelry.

The sauce and spaghetti flew high above the table, in a perfect arc. It was like a shooting star, a comet. One hundred pairs of eyes watched its shocking, scandalous trail. It lobbed up high, it plunged toward the earth, its tail streaming behind it.

And it landed—*smack*—on the top of the boy's jet-black hair.

Red sauce leaped upward before spilling down his cheek and neck. Long strands of spaghetti flexed and flopped and lay like long white worms on top of his Perfecto hair.

Sam bowed. "Mr. Peanut Butter," he said, "sends his compliments."

And for a moment he felt wonderful.

FIFTEEN

SAM SAW THE CHIEF judge holding his head in his hands.

He looked up to the gallery and saw red-faced Muriel and ghost-white George.

He looked to the Perfecto Kiddos. They sat with their knives and their forks in their hands and their mouths wide open.

Nancy pushed her chair back. Her dress was drenched and probably ruined. She had a shocked, smiling look on her face. She touched his arm and began to say something, but then Sam heard his mother's voice, calling from the gallery.

"Sam Kellow, don't you move!"

He looked toward the gallery, at all the staring silent

grown-up faces. His mother and his father were hurrying down the stairs into the ballroom.

Sam watched them come toward him. He felt so sad and sorry. No one would believe the grand plans he had had. All they would see was that he had behaved badly.

On his right he could hear Gloria sobbing.

But now his mother and his father were *running* across the ballroom. The three judges put their score-cards to one side and stared open-mouthed.

There was no hope. Everything was lost completely. The public-address system made a spluttering, laughing sound. Then a voice boomed:

"Perfecto Boy thirty-two, Perfecto Girl thirty-two, present yourselves immediately at the judges' podium."

"You're dead, Mr. Peanut," said the boy with the jet-black hair. "You are totally *executed*."

SIXTEEN

PHILLIP LOPATE DID not want to be a judge.

But he had signed a contract when he agreed to play the part of a general in his most recent film, *Invasion Force.* This contract had two signatures on every page except the last, which had six signatures on it. In this contract he had promised not just to learn his lines and act in the movie, but to do "all things possible" to promote it afterward.

So if the film company told him to go to a shopping mall and draw marbles out of a barrel for a contest, he had to go. If they told him to get up at four in the morning to appear on a TV talk show, he had no choice but to do it. And if they told him he had to fly to Toronto in the middle of a snowstorm and judge some dumb contest for Perfecto Kiddo (whatever that was), he had to do as he was told. And so he had packed his bag and gone to Toronto and tried to be pleasant to everyone.

But it was so hard to be pleasant when the very idea of the contest made him want to throw up.

The representatives of the Perfecto Company who had met him at the hotel were humorless and self-important. They showed him a tape of the Perfecto Kiddo commercials before they showed him to his room. He hated the commercials. They made his skin crawl.

Finally, he had escaped from the Perfecto executives and stepped into an elevator full of kids who reeked of soap, shampoo, and perfume. They were Perfecto Kiddos and he was embarrassed to be a part of their exploitation.

Phillip Lopate had kids of his own, a boy and a girl who were now grown up. He liked kids, the way they are in real life. But this bunch . . . it was hard for him to even look at them without his feelings showing in his face.

And so he took his place on the judges' podium feeling nauseous. He pretended to make notes, but all he was doing was making doodles on his pad, and that was what he was occupied with when he first noticed Sam Kellow walking into the hall.

Phillip Lopate was an actor, and actors are always thinking about different walks for when they need to use them in their acting. It didn't take the old movie star long to figure out why the kid walked the way he did—his shoes were tight. Also his jacket was too small—it affected how he swung his arms.

He peeked sideways at the scorecards of his fellow judges. The woman with all that jewelry (was her name Delia or Deborah? he forgot) had already marked a minus two next to boy number thirty-two. This made Phillip Lopate like boy number thirty-two. He was interesting to watch.

He watched Sam Kellow try to dance. He saw two things—that he had not danced before, but also that he had some talent. He liked his attitude. He gave him three out of three for dancing. He was the chief judge; he could do it if he wanted to.

He watched the girl. The girl was nice to the boy and the actor liked her because of it. He thought about how grown-ups had pushed these kids into this situation and he did not like the grown-ups for doing that. If there had been a score for grown-ups, it would have been a minus. He gave the girl three out of three for her attitude. He was starting to have a good time.

He was supposed to watch *all* the children, of course, but he found that rather painful to do. He had two judges, both very serious product managers from the Perfecto Company, one on either side of him, and these two earnest folk were going to tell him who should win, according to their scoring.

He would have preferred to have been at La Fenice lunching with his grown-up son. But he was obliged to stay, and so he got his pleasure from watching Sam Kellow.

When the spaghetti comet flew across the air, the chief judge laughed out loud, right into his microphone. "Ha-ha!" He had not meant to, but he was so astonished, so shocked, so pleased, really—that was the truth—to see someone do the sort of thing he would have liked to do himself.

Have you ever heard Phillip Lopate's voice? It's big and deep and when he laughed at Sam Kellow into his microphone, the laugh boomed out across the ballroom, as loud as rolling thunder.

He saw Sam look at him. He saw his hurt face. He was

so sorry he had laughed. He felt his embarrassment. He would have done anything to take that laugh back.

Then there was a great commotion as the child's parents ran across the floor. Phillip Lopate thought, They're upset he's not going to win. He shook his big lion's mane and scowled.

And yet when he looked at the parents, he could not dislike them. He liked how they hugged their boy, how they smiled and laughed and wept.

Beside him Deborah (or was it Deidre?) sniffed. "That's not Wilfred," she said. "He's number thirty-two but he's not Wilfred Mifflin."

"Those are not Wilfred Mifflin's parents," said the other judge. "What will I do? They're impostors."

"Give me your scores," said Phillip Lopate.

They both looked at him and hesitated.

"I am the chief judge," said the actor. He was already acting. He was speaking like the army commander in *Invasion Force.*

"Yes, sir," said the judge in the blue suit.

"Give me your scores," said Phillip Lopate. He was the army commander still. "And I will make my decision."

"*Your* decision?" asked the judge with the gold jewelry.

"I am the chief judge," said Phillip Lopate. "Isn't that what you told me? You make your recommendation to me. But I am the one who makes the final decision."

"Yes, but it is customary for the chief judge to endorse our recommendations."

"It is customary for me," the actor said, using a line he had had to learn for *Invasion Force,* "it is customary for me to do things my way."

"Yes, *sir,*" said the judges.

Phillip Lopate rose to his feet. Suddenly he was feeling very good.

"Perfecto Boy thirty-two," he called, "Perfecto Girl thirty-two, present yourselves."

SEVENTEEN

"YOU DON'T HAVE TO go," his mum said. His dad held Sam's hand firmly and looked him in the eye. "We can walk right out of here," he said. "You don't have to do a thing."

But Nancy was already standing up. She was drenched, bedraggled. As she began to walk across to the podium, a nasty buzz of whispering rose up inside the ballroom.

"It's okay, Dad," Sam said.

He had to go with Nancy. This mess was all his responsibility. It was his fault she was being whispered about by all her so-called friends, by all their parents up in the gallery.

Sam looked up at the gallery, and there she was. Muriel. She stared down at Sam with her wild and angry bright blue eyes swimming behind her spectacles.

"Up here," the chief judge's voice boomed out across the ballroom. "One culprit on each side of me."

It seemed like the judges' podium was a mile away. And once he was there, there were steps to climb and wires to trip on. Finally, Sam sat down in the chair next to the chief judge. It was like some kind of dreadful nightmare. The judge put his big brown hand across the microphone. Up in the gallery George lifted his two hands in the air and wrung them, as if he was twisting Sam's neck.

"Now," the judge whispered to Sam, "what's your real name?"

"Sir?" Sam was looking at George. He had put his long white fingers around his own neck and was throttling himself.

"What is it? Your real name."

"Sam Kellow."

"Not Wilfred Mifflin?"

"No, sir."

"Your parents here?"

Sam pointed to the table where he had disgraced

himself. His father sat in Sam's wet chair, his mother in Nancy's, while Sam and Nancy sat up here, on the podium, in their dripping clothes.

Sam looked down and found, on the desk in front of him, the scorecards the Perfecto product managers had left in plain view.

There was one chart for boys and one for girls. Sam looked at his number. This judge had given him minus two for dancing, minus four for deportment. Then she had written *Disgrace*.

"Good evening, ladies, gentlemen, children," boomed the voice of the chief judge. "My name is Phillip Lopate and when you first saw me tonight I was not pleased to be here."

At this point Sam stopped listening. He heard the big voice booming out, but he could not bear to listen to the words. He could not look at his parents, either. He shivered inside his wet clothes and looked at that big word *Disgrace*.

"I was pretending to be pleased," the chief judge said, "but as many of you know, I am an actor. Now, however, I am in the happy position of saying what I really think. Ladies and gentlemen, I have seen the Perfecto Kiddo, or rather, two of them. Look at them," he said.

He was looking at Sam and Nancy, but Sam had his head bowed and did not notice. *Disgrace,* he thought, that's right.

"If by 'perfecto,' we mean to suggest perfect, then these look pretty perfecto to me," the chief judge said. "These are not fake. These are the real McCoy. No one would mistake them for adults. They have been into mischief. They have messed up their hair. One has spaghetti sauce on his face. Who cares?" the judge boomed. "WHO CARES? I have seen smiles on these two faces that would, in the words of the great poet, light up the heavens.

"Ladies and gentlemen, I announce the winners of the Perfect Kiddo Competition to be Sam Kellow and Nancy See."

There was a shriek from the gallery. A great dreadful shriek of rage. It was so dreadful that Sam's mother never forgot it. It was what Sam's mum and dad mentioned first when they told the story of the day Sam Kellow was called a Perfecto Kiddo—the sound of Muriel shrieking as she rose unsteadily into the air above the gallery.

Five feet she rose, shrieking, pointing with her finger at Sam Kellow.

Sam could tell the story, too, but the truth was he didn't see the whole of Muriel's ascent. When he finally realized he had won the Big Bazoohley, he fainted and fell off his chair. He did not see Muriel's flight come to a dead stop as she bumped her head against the gallery ceiling. He therefore missed her curse, her fall, her broken leg. Indeed, he could never quite believe it had happened.

By the time he woke, Muriel had been rushed to the hospital. Sam had also been carried from the ballroom. When he awoke, he was lying on a sofa in a strange room with soft light. Nancy was bending over him, holding a piece of pink paper. On it was written "Pay to the order of Sam Kellow Ten Thousand Dollars."

EIGHTEEN

By the time Sam's mother found her son again, she did not really care where Mr. de Vere was. She had her son, and that was all that mattered. Sooner or later she would find someone else to buy her painting.

When Sam went to the black-suited cashiers and paid the hotel bill, she was proud of him. When he phoned the private detective in the Yellow Pages, she was amazed at how grown-up he had become. But when he announced that he was taking his mum and dad out to dinner, she burst into tears and kissed him.

Vanessa Kellow put on her best evening dress and carried the embroidered clutch bag that had belonged to her mother. Earl put on his tux.

The snowstorm had finally ended and all of Toronto was out again in the bustling streets, all bundled up against the cold. Sam and his mother and father took the subway to Osgoode and walked beside the six-foot snowbanks to a cozy little restaurant on King Street.

When Sam saw that Nancy and her parents were sitting at the next, table, he felt the happiest he could ever remember.

This was chance. Completely chance. But before long they had pushed the tables together, and then they were all talking about Jamaica and looking at the bro-

chures Nancy had brought for her parents, and by the time they had finished the main course, they were all planning to take the trip together.

And then Sam's mother gave a little squeal and stood up, holding her napkin across her mouth.

Sam turned and saw three people standing at the doorway. The first two he knew—the judges from the Perfecto competition: the young man in the navy-blue suit and the older woman with all that clanking jewelry. But when he saw the third person, the hair on his neck stood on end.

"Mr. de Vere!" his mother cried.

Could this peculiar little person be the famous Mr. de Vere? The man who was now emerging from the huge black fur coat had a long snouty face and soft gray eyes. He was shorter than Sam and he was dressed in a gray striped suit which revealed the curve of a splendid little belly. As he handed over his coat, he perched a small pair of wire-framed spectacles on the tip of his shining black nose.

"Mr. de Vere," Vanessa said, half whispering.

She was interrupted by the man in the navy-blue suit pointing his finger at Sam. "That's him," he hissed to Mr. de Vere. But Mr. de Vere was looking at Sam's mother and shaking his head.

"Vanessa," he said, "thank heavens!" He was now smiling broadly. Just behind him, the judges were furious—snapping and squalling like seabirds.

"It wasn't a majority decision," said judge number one.

"It has to be a majority decision," judge number two said. "The rules state it clearly."

But Mr. de Vere was not listening to the Perfecto judges. He was walking toward Sam's mother, his small jeweled hands outstretched. "I want my beautiful painting," he said. "I want it now."

"You weren't there," Sam's mother said to Mr. de Vere. "We all searched for you, but your door wasn't there."

"My dear, I sent you a change-of-address card in Australia."

"But we weren't in Australia," Earl Kellow said. "We've been traveling, Eddie."

"Mr. de Vere," said the female judge, pushing forward and pointing at Sam. "That's him, the party who was wrongly given the prize."

"This is not a *party,*" said Vanessa. And she put her hands on Sam's shoulders and held him as if someone wished to steal him from her. "This is my son, Sam Kellow."

Mr. de Vere pushed his wire-framed spectacles all the way back from the end of his nose to his small, mild, blinking eyes.

As Mr. de Vere studied him, Sam could smell a damp earth smell, not dirty, but really rather nice-smelling.

"This is the villain who won my contest?" Mr. de Vere asked at last.

"Yes, that's the boy," said the woman. "That's the girl, too. Drinking that red drink."

But Mr. de Vere did not look at Nancy, only at Sam.

“Ha-ha . . .” he said. He clapped his small jeweled hands together. “Your son,” he said, smiling at Vanessa. “The very woman I’ve been looking for everywhere. And it is your son that is causing this catastrophe in my business. My people are upset,” he said to Earl.

“Your *people*?” Earl Kellow said.

“My Perfecto product managers, my marketing people.”

“You don’t own Perfecto,” said Earl. “You *don’t*.”

“Who else, kiddo? I didn’t get rich licking stamps. My people were furious. You know, young fellow,” the odd little man said to Sam, “you’ve just ruined my entire worldwide marketing plan.”

“That Perfecto Kiddo stuff is yours, Eddie?” Earl could hardly believe it.

“It is the source of all my wealth.”

“It’s kind of disgusting, isn’t it, Eddie? Did you ever meet the parents?”

“Well,” said Mr. de Vere, “I do admit that many of the contestants are not my sort of people. . . . But then, who is?”

He looked at Sam, blinking rapidly. Sam could not stop staring at him. He was so odd. He looked like nothing so much as a mole. Indeed, when you studied him closely, you could see that he had soft, sleek gray fur all over his face.

"I myself," said Mr. de Vere, looking down at the backs of his own small furry hands, "am hardly perfecto."

There was a long sad silence in the room.

"You are warm and alive," Vanessa said at last. "You are curious and intelligent and you have a great eye. That's what perfecto should mean—not name-dropping and meanness and cheating."

"Sadly," said Mr. de Vere, "sadly, people are affected by one's appearance."

The silence this time was shorter.

"Not so deeply as they are by kindness," said Vanessa firmly, "or courage. Mr. de Vere, this is my son, Sam. He went off to find you, in his *sleep,* and then he was kidnapped, and then he set out to make the money his family needed."

Mr. de Vere put out his strange little hand and patted Sam on the shoulder. Sam looked at the glistening gold rings and smelled the damp earth smell again.

"If it was up to me, Vanessa, the Perfecto commercials wouldn't be like this."

"But it is up to you. You own the company."

"It is just that he isn't the *type* our customers would identify with," said the man in the navy-blue suit.

"He is the *type* who would chance everything for his family," said Earl. "Who wouldn't want to identify with that?"

"I would," said Mr. de Vere, looking suddenly sentimental, wiping a tear from his furry gray cheek. "Oh yes, I would. There is nothing to beat that. Not anything." He looked at the two judges and seemed to be waiting for their comments.

"In human terms," said the man from Perfecto, "who could argue?"

"In *human* terms," said the woman, and she suddenly blew her nose.

"Well," said Vanessa, "that is what I'd like to think, too. Sam took a big chance. That's what life is, don't you think, Mr. de Vere? You absolutely have to take a chance."

"Oh, life is a gamble," said Mr. de Vere. "There is no doubt about it. Love, business, art—you have to take a chance. You took a chance," he said to Sam, "and it seems . . ." He looked at Vanessa and then at the floor. "It seems . . . well, it does appear that he has won." He looked over his shoulder toward the judges. "In human terms," he said, his eyes twinkling.

Sam's dad put his hands under his son's arms and lifted him high into the air. "That's my boy," he said. "You won the Big Bazoohley. When things are bad, it's sometimes hard to believe the bad times are ever going to end, but then, *pow,* here we are, the Big Bazoohley. You're on a winning streak, my boy." Earl Kellow snapped his fingers and pointed to the kitchen door. "I bet you something good comes out that door."

As the fingers snapped, a waiter came out, bearing a beautiful Bombe Alaska on a silver tray.

"You see." He snapped his fingers again. (He was such a great finger-snapper. He made a noise like a whip crack.) And then the restaurant lights were dimmed and the waiter lit a sparkler and the Bombe Alaska burst briefly into flame, and Nancy leaned across and squeezed Sam's hand under the table, and his mother smiled at him, and the grown-ups stood and held their glasses high to the two kids.

"To the Big Bazoohley," they said, even the two judges.

Then everyone ate cake.

EPILOGUE

IF YOU EVER SEE *Toronto in a Matchbox,* you will want to find Mr. de Vere. It isn't easy. You won't find him quickly, but he is there, peeking out at you from a curtained window on King Street. He's the small, kindly but snouty-faced man in the window of a restaurant called La Fenice. He has a large white handkerchief in his hand and he is using it to wipe a tiny piece of Bombe Alaska from the tip of his small black nose.

If you look through the chink in the curtain with your magnifying glass, you will see a celebration in progress: Sam and Nancy side by side, Earl and Vanessa dancing cheek to cheek.

Muriel, of course, is in the painting, too, but not (thank heavens!) in the restaurant. She is in three different places in the painting. She is standing in the gallery above the ballroom. She is outside the hotel being helped into an ambulance. She is in a helicopter rising up above the snowbound city. If you look closely at the helicopter with that magnifying glass, you will see not only two unhappy grown-up faces but one very happy kid's face as well: It is Wilfred sitting beside the pilot, wearing his Blue Jays cap.

Where are Muriel and George and Wilfred going?

The painting does not tell you.

Is Wilfred about to begin a happier life? Will anyone ever let him take a chance?

No one can be certain, but from that day forward there were never any more Perfecto Kiddo competitions, and to that extent the world that Wilfred lived in was a much, much better place.

PETER CAREY

is the Booker Prize-winning author of *Oscar and Lucinda, Illywhacker,* and most recently, *The Unusual Life of Tristan Smith.* Born in Australia, he now makes his home with his wife and two sons, Sam and Charley, in New York City.

He says about the book: "One night in Toronto, my son Sam sleepwalked out of our hotel room. We were sound asleep and didn't hear him knocking. That's how *The Big Bazoohley* was born. The book is scarier, happier, and funnier than the real adventure."

The Big Bazoohley is Mr. Carey's first book for children.